Mr Cree
the Cr

by ALLAN AHLBERG

with pictures by
ANDRÉ AMSTUTZ

PUFFIN

PUFFIN BOOKS

Published by the Penguin Group
Penguin Books Ltd, 80 Strand, London WC2R 0RL, England
Penguin Group (USA), Inc., 375 Hudson Street, New York, New York 10014, USA
Penguin Books Australia Ltd, 250 Camberwell Road, Camberwell, Victoria 3124, Australia
Penguin Books Canada Ltd, 10 Alcorn Avenue, Toronto, Ontario, Canada M4V 3B2
Penguin Books India (P) Ltd, 11 Community Centre, Panchsheel Park, New Delhi – 110 017, India
Penguin Group (NZ), cnr Airborne and Rosedale Roads, Albany, Auckland 1310, New Zealand
Penguin Books (South Africa) (Pty) Ltd, 24 Sturdee Avenue, Rosebank 2196, South Africa

Penguin Books Ltd, Registered Offices: 80 Strand, London WC2R 0RL, England

puffinbooks.com

First published 1988
35 34

Text copyright © Allan Ahlberg, 1988
Illustrations copyright © André Amstutz, 1988

Educational Advisory Editor: Brian Thompson

Manufactured in China

Filmset in Century Schoolbook (Linotron 202) by
Rowland Phototypesetting (London) Ltd

British Library Cataloguing in Publication Data
A CIP catalogue record for this book is available from the British Library

ISBN–13: 978–0–14032–345–0

Mr Creep the crook was a bad man.
Mrs Creep the crook was a bad woman.
Miss Creep and Master Creep
were bad children,
and "Growler" Creep was a bad dog.

For some of the time Mr Creep
and his family lived in a secret den.
For the rest of the time
they lived in jail.

One day Mr Creep was sitting
in his little jail-house.
He was drinking a cup of jail-house tea
and eating a piece of jail-house cake
and planning how to get out.

Here is Mr Creep's plan.

Mrs Creep was knitting a jail-house jumper.
When she saw the plan, she said,
"That's a nice plan – can we stop
at a wool shop?"
"And a sweet shop, too!" the children said.
But Mr Creep shook his head.
"No," he said. "No changes to the plan –
it's fool-proof!"

A few weeks later, this happened.
As you can see, the plan
was fool-proof – well, nearly.

The next day
Mr Creep was sitting on the sand.
He was eating a seaside sandwich,
and drinking a bottle of seaside beer
and planning how to get-rich-quick.

Bike

Seaside

Here is Mr Creep's plan.

Who to rob

What to take

Mr Biff

gloves

Mr Cosmo

Magic Hat

Mrs Wobble

Food

Mrs Creep was being buried
in the sand by the children.
When she saw the plan, she said,
"That's a *very* nice plan –
but you forgot the wool shop!"

Then, a few days later, this happened.

The Creeps got biffed
by Mr Biff,

and had their bottoms burned
by Mrs Plug.

Mr Cosmo the conjuror
played a trick on them.

Mrs Wobble the waitress
dropped a jelly on them.

They got stung by bees,

kicked by a horse and chased by cops.

By mistake, they also burgled
a burglar – and *he* robbed *them*!
And besides all that – it snowed.

"Was that a fool-proof plan, too, dad?"
the children said.
And Mr Creep said, "No."

A few hours later
Mr Creep was sitting in his secret den.
He was drinking a glass of secret water,
and sticking a secret plaster on his nose.
Also, he was dreaming
of his cosy jail-house ...
and planning how to get back *in*!
Here is Mr Creep's plan.

Seaside

Stolen car

Getting 'Back in' plan

"This time it really is
a fool-proof plan," he said.
And it was.

Now, as you have seen,
Mr Creep the crook was a bad man.
Mrs Creep the crook was a bad woman.
Miss Creep and Master Creep
were bad children,
and "Growler" Creep was a bad dog.

However, most things change,
as time goes by.
So, after a year or two,
the Creeps were not quite so bad.
And after another year,
they were nearly good.
And after six more months,
they *were* good.

At last they were let out of jail.

The next day
Mr Creep was sitting up in bed.
He was drinking a cup of home-made coffee
and eating a slice of home-made toast
and planning his last plan.

Being good — final plan

Mr Creep   get a job   Lollipop Man

Mrs Creep   get a job   WOOL Dept   Sales Lady

Master & Miss Creep   go to School   Top of class

Growler   well trained

When Mrs Creep and the children
saw the plan, they said,
"That's the best plan of all!"
"It's perfect, dad!"
"It's fool-proof!"
And so it was...

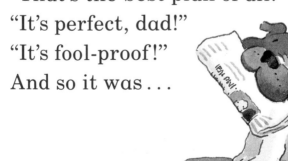

... well, nearly.

The End